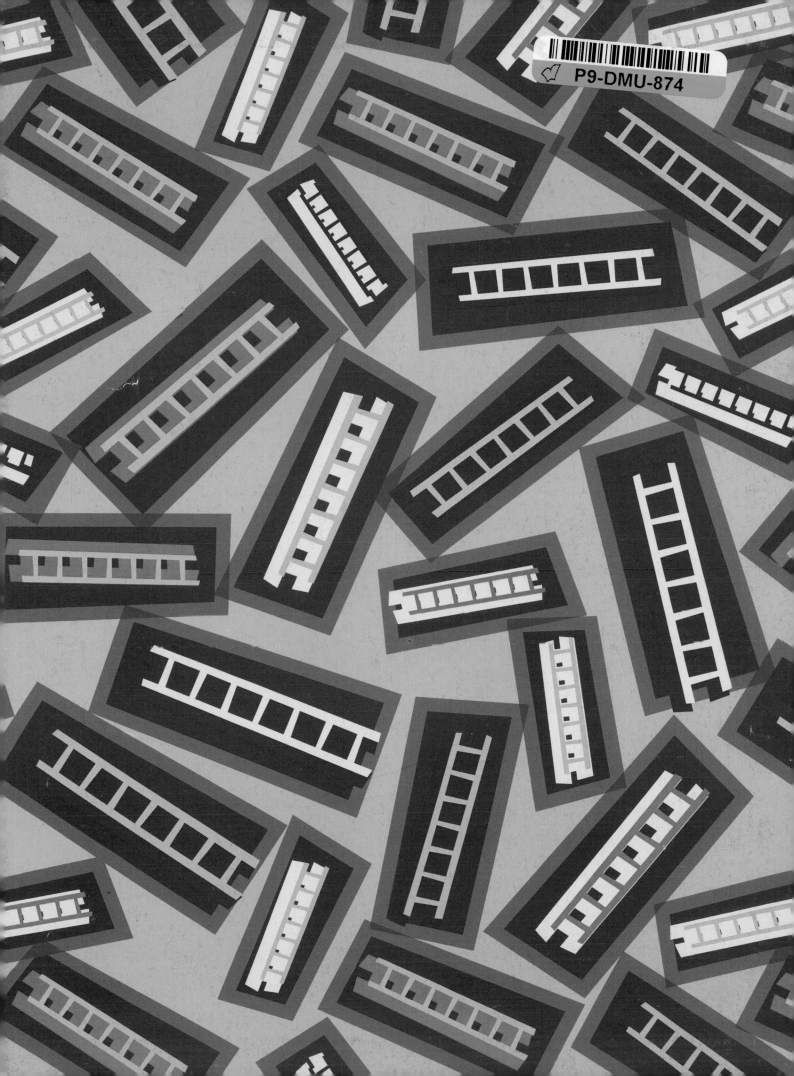

EGMONT
We bring stories to life

First published in Great Britain 2011 by Egmont UK Ltd
239 Kensington High Street, London W8 6SA

ISBN 978 0 6035 6637 0
1 3 5 7 9 10 8 6 4 2
Printed in Italy

Fireman Sam™

Story Treasury

8 Stories

Contents

Bug-eyed boy from Venus

One dark night, Fireman Sam was showing Sarah, James and Norman how to use his telescope.

"Point it over there," said Sam. "To the planet Venus ..."

"Venus!" said Norman. "Bug-eyed monsters live there!"

Just then, a bright light lit up the sky. "It's a shooting star," said Sam.

"No! That was an alien spaceship," said Norman. "From Venus!"

Next day, when James, Sarah and Norman were on their way to school Norman spotted a crop circle. "Look, it's where the aliens landed!" he told them.

"There's no such thing as aliens," said Trevor Evans, the bus driver.

"We'll see about that," whispered Norman.

After school, Norman went to Bella's café. He covered his face in green mushy peas and put on a silver foil cape and helmet.

"Arrrrrrr!" wailed Norman in his best alien voice.

"Arrrrrrr!"

News of the "alien" soon spread. When Trevor saw it heading for Pontypandy Mountain he told James and Sarah.

"Come on!" said James. "We'll catch him!"

Norman was running along when he slipped off the path into a muddy bog. He tried to get out, but he sank deeper and deeper into the black mud.

"**HELP!**" he cried, as Trevor and the twins arrived.

"HELP!"

"I'm stuck!" cried Norman. "Get me out of here!"

Back at the shop, Dilys was so worried about Norman that she rang 999. "My Norman's been taken by aliens!" she reported.

Sam got the message, pressed the alarm and the bell started ringing. "Aliens?" he said. "Likely story! But we'd better send out a search party."

Jupiter and the Fire Station crew were soon out on the road and at the Mountain Rescue Station Tom Thomas lifted off in the helicopter.

ACTION STATIONS!

Trevor knew how dangerous the bog was. He lay flat and told Sarah and James to hold on to his legs as he stretched out his hand to Norman.

"Hurry up, Mr Evans," said Norman. "My pants are filling up with mud!"

"It's no good, I'm sinking!" said Trevor. "Pull me back! We need help!"

As he spoke, the helicopter's blades whirred above them and a searchlight swept the sky.

"Over here!" cried Trevor.

Minutes later, Tom winched Sam up into the air then lowered him down over the bog. Norman was very pleased to see him!

Sam put a harness under Norman's arms. "I've got him!" he shouted to Tom. "Take it away!"

The helicopter rose up into the dark sky, with Sam and Norman in tow.

"SQUELCH!" went Norman as he was pulled free from the mud.

Dilys and Bella were waiting in the park when they saw the helicopter's lights.

"It's the spaceship that took my Norman!" said Dilys.

Seconds later a strange shape appeared in the darkness.

"It's-a hideous!" said Bella. "It's-a terrifying! It's-a ..."

"NORMAN!" said Dilys as he and Sam stepped out of the shadows.

"Yes, one green alien, safe and sound!" said Sam.

"My little precious!" said Dilys, giving Norman a big kiss.

"Oh, Mam!" said Norman. "Yuk!"

King of the jungle

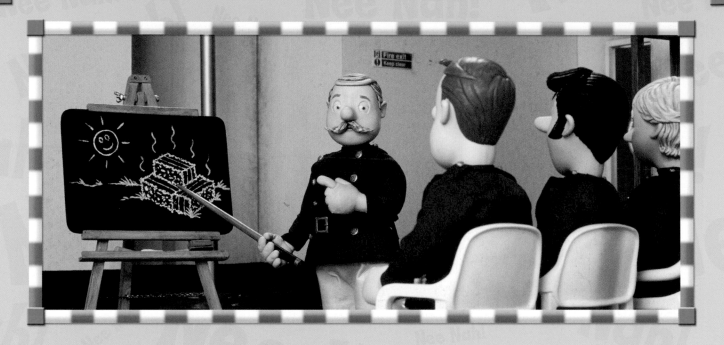

It was summer in Pontypandy. Station Officer Steele was telling the firefighters about how things can burst into flames all by themselves. "It can happen to haystacks in very hot weather," he said. "A warning sign is if the hay smells like toffee."

At the shop, Norman put on his mum's furry bath mat so he looked like Tarzan. **"Aaa-eee-aaa-eee-aaa!"** he yelled.

Sarah and James were pretending to be knights. They had wooden swords and shields.

"Hi, Norman!" said Sarah.

Norman pretended he hadn't heard them.

"You need to wash your ears out," yelled Sarah. **"HI, NORMAN!"**

"Ow, that hurt!" said Norman. "Who you shout at?" he said in a deep voice. "Me not Norman, me Narzan, king of jungle!"

Mandy arrived. "Does your mam know you're wearing her bath mat?" she asked.

"Me no got mam," said Norman. "Me live with gorillas."

He took a banana from outside the shop and ate it. Then he tossed the skin away.

Trevor was delivering a box of tomatoes. He slipped on the banana skin and fell, **ooof!** The tomatoes flew into the air and landed – **splat!** – on James and Sarah.

"Aargh!" said James.

"Yuck!" said Sarah.

"Me sorry," said Norman.

James was cross. "We're going to play knights and you're not invited!" he said.

"Me no want play," said Norman. "Me Narzan, you tomato-heads!"

Norman and Mandy went to the park.

Norman swung on a rope swing. **"Aaa-eee-aaa-eee-aaa-eee-aaa!"** he cried.

"Aaa-eee-aaa-eee-aaa!"

"Can I have a go?" asked Mandy.

"No! You go find nanas for Narzan!" said Norman.

"Get your own nanas!" said Mandy.

"I'm not playing!"

"Narzan no need you," said Narzan.

"Animals are his friends. Woolly! Dusty! Come!"

"Baa!" said Woolly.

"Woof!" said Dusty.

Norman went off with them. "We go to jungle!"

Out in the fields, the twins found a scarecrow to join their game.

"We are brave knights," said James. "We will attack the castle of evil Baron Blackheart!"

"What castle?" asked Sarah.

James pointed to a stack of hay bales. "That one!"

They fought the scarecrow and threw it to the ground.

Sarah sniffed. "What's that yummy smell?" she said. "It's like …"

"Toffee!" said James, taking a bag from his pocket. "It must be these. Want one?"

The twins didn't see that wisps of smoke were coming from the top of the haystack!

At the Fire Station, Sam was showing Elvis his new invention. "You stick the broom handle into haystacks. The thermometer on the end tells you how hot they are."

Elvis stuck it into his pasta. "Well, my spaghetti's hot stuff!" he said.

Norman wanted Dusty and Woolly to play jungle animals. But they just wanted to chase their tails!

Suddenly Dusty stopped and sniffed. "Woof!"

"You smell trouble?" said Norman. He sniffed. "Me do too!"

He looked around and saw the twins playing near the haystack. It was on fire! "Get away from the haystack!" he yelled.

James saw Norman. "Look, he's waving at us," he said.

"Take no notice!" said Sarah. "I've still got tomato bits in my hair thanks to him!"

Norman had to get help. He raced off to raise the alarm.

"Stop!" he cried when he saw Nurse Flood in her car. "It's the twins! There's a fire!"

"This is a job for Fireman Sam," said Nurse Flood. "I'll call him on my mobile."

"Great Fires of London!" said Sam when he got the message. "We've got a hot haystack on our hands!"

Sam, Elvis and Penny put on their helmets and jumped aboard Jupiter. The blue lights flashed and the siren wailed – **Nee Nah! Nee Nah!** They raced off at full speed.

The twins were still playing when bits of burning hay started to fall on them. "Run!" said Sarah.

James tripped and hurt his ankle, but Jupiter arrived seconds later.

Sam moved the twins to safety while Penny and Elvis hosed down the flames until the fire was out.

Sam pushed the broom handle invention into the haystack. "It's cool now," he said. "It's safe."

Later on, Sarah and James thanked Norman for raising the alarm.

Narzan beat his fists on his chest. **"Aaa-eee-aaa-eee-aaa-eee-aaa!"** he said. **"Me brave Narzan!"**

"Aaa-eee-aaa-eee-aaa!"

Carnival of Junk

One morning, Mike and Helen Flood were sitting down to breakfast. They were talking about going on holiday to Jamaica.

But when Mandy walked into the kitchen, they stopped talking, and stared. Her face was covered in **big red spots!**

Helen is the Pontypandy nurse, so she knew what the spots meant! "You've got chickenpox, Mandy," she said. "You'll have to stay at home for at least two weeks."

"But what about our holiday in Jamaica?" said Mandy. "That means I won't be able to go to the big carnival!"

"I know," said Helen. "It's a shame, but we'll just have to cancel the holiday and go next year, instead."

"Oh, it's not fair!" said Mandy, sadly.

"Sorry," said Helen. "Come on, it's back to bed for you, I'm afraid."

Helen came back downstairs and spoke to Mike. "Mandy's very upset," she said. "I wish there was some way we could make it

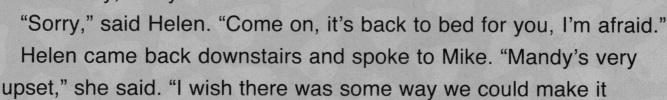

up to her."

Mike thought for a second or two. "There is!" he said. "If we can't take Mandy to the carnival, we'll bring the carnival to Mandy!"

He got out his mobile phone and rang the café.

"Hello, Bella, Mike here," he said. "Do you know any Caribbean recipes? You do? **Fantastic!**"

That afternoon, Sarah and James went to visit Fireman Sam at the Fire Station. He was with Penny and Elvis, trying out a new metal-cutter called the Jaws of Life.

"Fancy a game of football, Uncle Sam?" asked Sarah.

Before Sam could reply, Station Officer Steele shook his head. "No football for your Uncle Sam today," he told the twins. "He's much too busy here. Now off you go, you two, and find something useful to do!"

"We will!" said James, and they rode off on their skateboards.

James went round a corner and skidded straight into a big pile of junk. There were bin bags, bits of broken furniture, and even a rusty old boiler.

"**What a mess!**" said James. "Someone must have dumped all this junk here."

"I think we've found something useful to do," said Sarah. "We can tidy it all up!"

"Good idea," said James. He pulled at a bag, but as he tugged, the big boiler rocked, bounced down, and knocked him over!

"**Ow!**" said James. "My leg's stuck under the boiler!"

"Don't move, James," said Sarah. "Your leg might be broken. I'll go to Bella's café and ring for help."

Meanwhile, Mandy was still in bed, reading a pony magazine. She didn't know that her mum and dad were making plans – carnival plans!

The other villagers were helping, too. Trevor and Norman were making balloons into animal shapes, and Bella was stirring a big pot of rice and peas.

Suddenly, Sarah ran in. "Can I use your phone, please, Bella?" she said. "It's an emergency!"

"**Mamma Mia!** Whas-a 'appen?" said Bella.

Sarah didn't have time to explain, and dialled 999. "Fire service, please!" she said. "**Hurry!**"

At the Fire Station, Penny read the message on the teleprinter. "Stand by, everyone!" she said. "A boy is stuck under a boiler."

"**Great Fires of London!**" said Sam. "Who is it?"

"It's James!" said Penny.

"**Action Stations!**" said Station Officer Steele.

Sam, Steele and Elvis put on their helmets and jumped on board Jupiter. The blue lights flashed, the siren wailed – **Nee Nah! Nee Nah!** – and they raced off. Penny was right behind them in Venus.

When they reached James, Dusty was looking after him!

Sam and Penny used the Jaws of Life to cut the big boiler into smaller pieces, and minutes later, James' leg was free.

"Stay clear of rubbish tips in future, James," said Sam. "They're full of hidden hazards."

"I will, Uncle Sam," said James.

Just then, Mike arrived. When he saw the boiler, he smiled. "That's just what we need, Sam," he said. "It's like this …"

Later on, Mandy heard steel band music. She looked out of her bedroom window and gasped in surprise. Sam was on Jupiter's platform and all her friends were outside, waving and dancing. Mike was playing a steel drum that Sam had made for him from what was left of the old boiler!

"**Wow!** It's just like the big carnival in Jamaica!" said Mandy, as her mum came into the bedroom.

"Yes," said Helen. "You can't go to Jamaica, so we brought the carnival to Pontypandy!"

"What are we waiting for, Mum?" said Mandy, happily. **"Let's dance!"**

Bath-time for Dusty

One day, Station Officer Steele was showing Fireman Sam a painting of a goat.
"That's Idris," Steele told him. "He was the mascot of my old army regiment."

"You know, **we** could do with a station mascot," said Sam.

"Yes," said Steele. "We'll have a mascot that's the pride of Pontypandy, a brave creature, the best beast in Wales! See to it will you, Sam?"

Sarah and James were petting Dusty the dog outside Dilys' shop when she put a notice in the window.

James read it. "Uncle Sam wants a mascot for the Fire Station," he said, looking at Dusty. "And we've got the perfect dog for the job!"

The twins took Dusty to the Fire Station.

"So you reckon Dusty would be the perfect mascot, do you?" said Sam.

30

"**Baaaaa!**"

As they were talking, Norman arrived with his pet sheep, Woolly.

"**Baaaaa!**" said Woolly.

"Norman," warned Sam, "if Station Officer Steele sees that lamb here, he'll ..."

"Make him your mascot!" said Norman, as Woolly jumped out of his arms and raced off.

They found him near the flower boxes at the Fire Station entrance.

"Great Fires of London!" said Sam. "He's gobbled up all our geraniums!"

"**Great fires of London!**"

When Station Officer Steele saw Woolly he said, "Get that sheepskin dustbin away from my station!"

Then he turned to Sam.

"Have you seen Mrs Lasagne's cat, Rosa?" he asked, putting his hand on the flower box. "Bella thinks she would make the perfect mascot."

"Weeeeeooooow!"

"Weeeeeooooow!" squealed Rosa, who had been fast asleep in the box.

"Yeeeeeooooow!" cried Steele as she scratched his hand. "That animal is disqualified!"

"Yeeeeeooooow!"

Sam winked at Sarah and James. "I think Dusty's got a good chance of being the mascot now," he said. "As long as he's cleaned up."

Sarah looked worried. "You mean Dusty needs a ..."

"BATH?" said James.

Sam nodded.

When Dusty saw the old tin bath James had filled with water, he whimpered and shook.

"Come on," James told him. "It's only water ..."

ONLY WATER! thought Dusty. What do you mean, **ONLY WATER?**

James held out a dog biscuit to tempt Dusty into the bath but he ran off with it and – **SPLOSH!** – it was James who ended up in the water!

SPLASH! SPLOSH!

Dusty ran away, knocked Norman off his skateboard and rode into the park on it. Then Dusty hit the fountain, soared into the air and landed – **OOF!** – on Trevor, who was taking a nap!

Then he ran off again.

OOF!

The twins chased after Dusty. They thought they'd lost him – when he popped his head out of a dustbin where he had been hiding and ran off again!

"After him!"

Dusty ran to the Mountain Rescue Station, where Mike Flood was repairing a boiler. But his blowtorch started a fire!

When Tom radioed Sam about the fire the alarm bell rang and Sam and Elvis put on their helmets and jumped aboard Jupiter. The blue lights flashed and the siren wailed – **Nee Nah! Nee Nah!** – as they raced to the Mountain Rescue Centre at full speed.

When the fire was out, Steele told the team to damp down the building with their hoses. Just then, Dusty thought it was safe to come out again and got a real soaking.

By the time James and Sarah arrived, water was dripping from his coat.

"Dusty got a bath, after all!" said Sarah.

A few days later, Dusty was dressed in his mascot's outfit. Sarah was trying to take a photograph, but Dusty kept looking away.

"Can someone make him look at the camera?" she asked.

James took a sausage out of his pocket and threw it up into the air. Dusty jumped for it, and when Sarah took the photo, Dusty was too close – and Sam wasn't in the picture at all!

"Oh, Dusty!" said Sam and the others. **"Woof!"** said Dusty.

"Woof!"

Trouble and squeak

One morning, Sam saw Norman carrying something covered in a blue cloth. "What have you got there?" he asked.

"This is the most daringest mouse in Pontypandy!" said Norman. "He can run up a ladder, dive through the air and land in a tub of cheese spread! Meet The Great Squeakendo!"

Mandy sighed. "He's Squeaky, the school mouse," she said. "Our teacher said Norman could look after him for the holidays."

Norman and Mandy took Squeaky to Norman's bedroom. They unrolled lots of rolls of toilet paper and taped the cardboard tubes together. They had made a maze for Squeaky!

Norman put a piece of cheese at one end. "Now, The Great Squeakendo will find his way through the Maze of Mystery!" he said.

But Squeaky's cage was empty. "Oh no!" said Norman. "He's escaped. Where is he?"

Later, Sam showed James and Sarah his latest invention. "It's a grabber," he told them. "The arms get longer so it can grab things that are too high to reach."

"Wow!" said James.

Back at the shop, Dilys was having a cup of tea when Squeaky peeped out of the biscuit tin. He was nibbling one of her biscuits!

"**Aaaaargh!**" said Dilys.

Upstairs, Norman and Mandy heard a noise outside. They looked out of the window and saw Dilys with a brush. She was sweeping Squeaky out into the street!

"Get out, you little pest!" said Dilys.

Mandy and Norman ran downstairs.

"That's not a pest, Mam," said Norman, as Squeaky ran off down the street. "He's the school pet! I'm looking after him!"

Oh!" said Dilys.

"Aaaaargh!"

Norman looked everywhere for Squeaky, but he couldn't find him. He made posters with Squeaky's picture on them and took one to the Fire Station. "His tail's bent and his ears stick out …" Norman told Sam. "I have to find him."

While Norman was at the Fire Station his teacher rang Dilys. She asked how Squeaky was getting on.

"Oh, he's fine," said Dilys. "Norman's … er … drawn pictures of him. Pinning them up all over town he is …"

Squeaky, meanwhile, went to Bella's café. He grabbed the cheese Bella was about to put on Trevor's pizza!

"Ai-ai-ai!" said Bella. "A giant-a rat! He steal-a my cheese!"

"That's no rat, it's The Great Squeakendo!" said Trevor. "His posters are all over town!"

Trevor tried to catch Squeaky, but he ran away.

Rosa leapt at him and chased him around the café.

"Hisssss!" said Rosa.

"Eeeek!" said Squeaky.

"Miaoow!"

Just then, Norman and Mandy arrived. "Squeaky!" said Norman. "Grab him!"

But Squeaky was too fast for them. He ran straight up the chimney, and so did Rosa!

"Squeak!" squeaked Squeaky.

"Miaoow!" howled Rosa.

"Oh, no. They're stuck up the chimney!" said Trevor.

"I'll call Fireman Sam," said Mandy.

When Sam arrived he put his new grabber up the chimney and gently grabbed Rosa.

"**MIAOW!**" said Rosa.

"I've got her!" said Sam.

When Rosa was out of the chimney, Squeaky ran down and Norman grabbed him.

"The Great Escaping Squeakendo!" said Norman. "I'm taking you home!"

When Norman got to the shop Dilys handed the phone to him. It was his teacher again.

"Yes, Miss," said Norman. "Squeaky's fine. We've been playing … er …"

"**Squeak!**" said Squeaky suddenly.

"That's right, hide and squeak!" smiled Norman.

"Squeak!"

Norman's Invisible Friend

One day, Norman was watching a TV programme about a boy who had an invisible friend. **"Cool!"** he said. "I'd like one of those."

Later on, Norman met Sarah and James.

"Guess what?" said Sarah. "Bella gave us an ice cream for helping in the café."

"Did she now?" said Norman. That gave him an idea!

Norman went to the café and cleared the tables.

Bella was amazed! "Why – thank-a you, Norman!" she said. "That's-a so kind! You deserve-a an ice cream. 'Ere you are."

"**Thanks!**" said Norman. "Er ... can my new friend Owain have one too? He's too shy to come in."

Bella gave Norman another ice cream, and he went off licking **both** of them.

"Invisible friends come in very useful!" he said.

At the Flood house, Nurse Flood was getting things ready for Mandy's birthday party when she was called out on a job.

"Here's what you need to do," she told Mike, giving him a list. **"See you later!"**

The first guests were Sarah and James. Their present for Mandy was a popcorn maker.

"Wicked!" said Mandy. "Dad, plug this in, please!"

"Sure," said Mike. "I'll do the toasties as well."

Mike was in a bit of a flap! He didn't notice that he had too many things plugged into the adaptor. And he didn't notice that it was starting to smoke!

The children were upstairs when Norman arrived and put a pair of shoes under the coat rack. "Whose are those?" said Mandy when she came downstairs.

"Er ... they're my new friend Owain's," said Norman. "He's in the bathroom."

"Oh," said Mandy. "Well, help yourselves to some food."

"I ... I mean ... **we** will," said Norman.

When Mike served up the food, Mandy sniffed. "I can smell burning, Dad," she said. "And now the smoke detector's going off!"

When Mike opened the kitchen door there was smoke everywhere! **"Everybody out!"** he said.

Mandy was on her way out when she saw Owain's shoes. "He must still be upstairs!" she told Sarah. "I'll go and get him."

Mike rang 999 and at the Fire Station, Elvis read out the emergency message. "There's a fire at Mike Flood's house!" he told the others.

"Action Stations!" said Station Officer Steele.

Sam, Steele and Elvis put on their helmets and jumped aboard Jupiter. The blue lights flashed, the siren wailed – **Nee Nah! Nee Nah!** – and they raced off. Penny was right behind them in Venus.

"Is everybody out?" Sam asked when they got to the house.

"No," said Sarah. "Mandy went upstairs to get Owain."

"Right," said Sam. "I'm going in!"

But as Sam went into the house, Norman stopped him.

"Owain isn't inside," he said. "He isn't anywhere. I made him up so I could get double helpings of things ..."

"But Mandy doesn't know that!" said Sam, going inside.

Sam soon found Mandy, and carried her downstairs. "But what about Owain?" she said.

"There is no Owain," said Sam. "Norman made him up."

When the fire was out, Sam explained what had happened. "You had too many things plugged into one socket, Mike," he said.

"I won't do it again, Sam," said Mike. "Now, let's carry on with the party at Bella's. Come on, Sam, Elvis, Penny, you're all invited."

At the party, Sam handed an empty glass to Norman.
"What's this?" asked Norman. **"Hey, where's my strawberry milkshake?"**
Sam grinned. "Your friend Owain must have drunk it!"

Fiery finale

Sam and Penny were helping Trevor get things ready for the Pontypandy Talent Show.

James was going to make animals from balloons.

Sarah was going to spin a plate on top of a long pole.

Mandy was going to do cartwheels.

But Norman couldn't decide on an act. "What about lion-taming with Rosa as my lion?" he said to Trevor. "Or fire-eating!"

Trevor shook his head. "I don't think so, Norman."

Tom helped Elvis set up his electric guitar. "Better get the amplifier under cover in case it rains," he said.

"Yeah, water and electricity don't mix," said Elvis.

Station Officer Steele arrived. "Cridlington!" he said. "What are you doing here? We can't all be in the show. Only one firefighter will represent the station … ME! Off you go!"

Norman was still trying to decide on an act. "What about a flea circus, Trevor?" he said. "I've trained Dusty's fleas to do tricks. Look, ready, steady – jump!"

When he heard the word 'flea', Trevor started to scratch! "Norman Price, stop that right now!" he said.

Norman was fed up. He sat down to read his cowboy comic. "Wish I could do tricks like Lasso Kid," he said. "I bet he'd win the show."

It started to rain, and soon there was a big puddle of water on the roof of the stage. But no one noticed …

Norman was watching rehearsals and picked up Elvis' guitar. "How do you turn it on?" he said. He flicked a switch. **Screech!** went the guitar. Norman fiddled with the amplifier. **SCREEEEEEECH!**

"My turn!" he said, running on stage. "I woke up this morning –
TWANG! – feeling really blue!" **SCREECH! TWANG!** "I didn't know
what to do!" Norman sang.

Trevor did! He put his hands over his ears, then grabbed the guitar.
"That's enough, Norman!" he said.

"But I want to be in the show!" said Norman. "What can I do?"

"I don't know," said Trevor. "Can't you rope someone in to help you?"

"Hmm …" said Norman. "Maybe I can!"

Station Officer Steele practised his song. "I'm a little teapot, short and
stout," he sang. "Here's my handle. Here's my spout."

Norman took no notice. He was untying one of the ropes that kept the
roof in place.

As Sarah started to spin a plate, Norman undid the rope and
yanked it free.

Whoosh! The water on the roof gushed down on to the stage! Water splashed on to the amplifier and it crackled and exploded, **whoomf!** Then the curtain burst into flames!

"Don't panic!" said Steele. "Trevor, call the station!"

At the Fire Station, Sam read the message. "We're going to the talent show, after all," he told Elvis and Penny. "The stage is on fire!"

Sam, Elvis and Penny put on their helmets. They jumped aboard Jupiter and the blue lights flashed. The siren wailed – **Nee Nah! Nee Nah!** – and they raced off to the park at full speed.

"Here's Jupiter now!" said Trevor. "Over here, Sam!"

Sam and Penny ran to the stage carrying the big hose. "Turn her on, Elvis!" called Sam.

Water whooshed out of the hose and soon the fire was out.

"Who switched that amplifier on?" asked Sam. "It's a very dangerous thing to do in this wet weather!"

"Sorry, Sam," said Norman.

When the talent show started, Norman's act was last.

"And now, the boy who made the West wild," said Trevor. "It's Lasso Kid Price and his clever coyote, Dusty!"

"Yee-ha!" said Norman. He spun his lasso into a big loop and Dusty leapt through it!

It was great! The crowd cheered and clapped. "More! More!"

"Well, there can only be one winner," said Trevor.

"Yee-ha!" said Norman. "Yeah, ME!"

"Yee-ha!"

Mummy's Little Pumpkin

It was Halloween, and Dilys' shop window was full of paper ghosts, witches' hats and plastic bats.

She was building a display of cans on the counter when Norman came downstairs. **"Wooo!"** he wailed, creeping up behind her.

"Now just because it's Halloween, it doesn't mean you have to go scaring everyone, Norman," said Dilys.

"It does if you're the **Scariest Vampire in Pontypandy**!" said Norman.

Norman opened the door. "I'm off now!" he said. "Count Norman leaves in search of the biggest pumpkin in the world!"

Norman slammed the door behind him, and poor Dilys' display crashed to the floor.

"It's going to be one of those days!" moaned Dilys.

In the Fire Station garden, Sarah and James were helping Fireman Sam pick some pumpkins when Norman arrived. "Looking for a pumpkin, Norman?" asked Sam, holding out a small one. "How about this one?" Norman shook his head, and grabbed the biggest pumpkin. "This one's perfect," he said. "It's a **monster**, like me!"

Sam smiled. "I hope you're not going to scare everyone like you did last year," he said.

"Oh no, I won't do that again," said Norman. "This year I'm going to be **even scarier**!"

Back at the shop, Norman carved the pumpkin into a lantern. But he left the squishy bits of pumpkin on the floor, and when Elvis walked in, he slipped on them, and fell. **CRASH!**

Down came Dilys' display of cans again!

"Sorry, Elvis," said Dilys. "It's just one of those days."

"Can I light my lantern now, Mam?" asked Norman.

"I'll do it for you," said Elvis. "You've got to be careful with candles. **Always** ask a grown-up to light them, and remember to blow them out before you go to bed."

"OK," said Norman.

Later on, Dilys went upstairs. "Keep an eye on that candle," she told Norman, as he put the lantern in the shop window.

That night, Count Norman the Vampire opened the door and looked outside. **"Tremble with fear, Count Norman is here!"** he said, slamming the door and running off.

In the shop, the pile of cans fell off the counter again, and the pumpkin lantern rolled on to the floor. The candle inside fell over and the wax started a fire!

James and Sarah were in Bella's café when they saw the fire.

"Quick!" said Sarah. "We have to call Uncle Sam!"

At the Fire Station, Sam read out the emergency message. "There's a fire at Dilys' shop!" he told the others.

"Action Stations!" said Station Officer Steele.

Sam, Steele and Elvis put on their helmets and jumped aboard Jupiter. The blue lights flashed, the siren wailed – **Nee Nah! Nee Nah!** – and they raced off. Penny was right behind them in Venus.

Norman got home just as Jupiter arrived. "I'll save you, Mam!" he called to Dilys.

"Don't worry, Norman," said Sam, stopping him. "Leave it to us."

Elvis and Penny pointed a hose at the shop window, and Sam went up on the rescue platform. **"Hold on, Dilys!"** he said.

Sam lifted Dilys on to the rescue platform, and it was lowered safely to the ground.

"Thanks, Sam. **You're a hero**," said Dilys.

She gave Norman a big hug. "And so are you, Norman. You tried to save me. **You're Mummy's brave little pumpkin**!"

Everyone went into Bella's café, and Sam showed Norman what was left of his pumpkin lantern.

"Remember, Norman, always be very careful with candles, and put your lantern somewhere where it won't fall over," said Sam.

"And don't slam doors!" added Dilys.

"I won't, I promise," said Count Norman the Vampire. **"Happy Halloween, everyone!"**

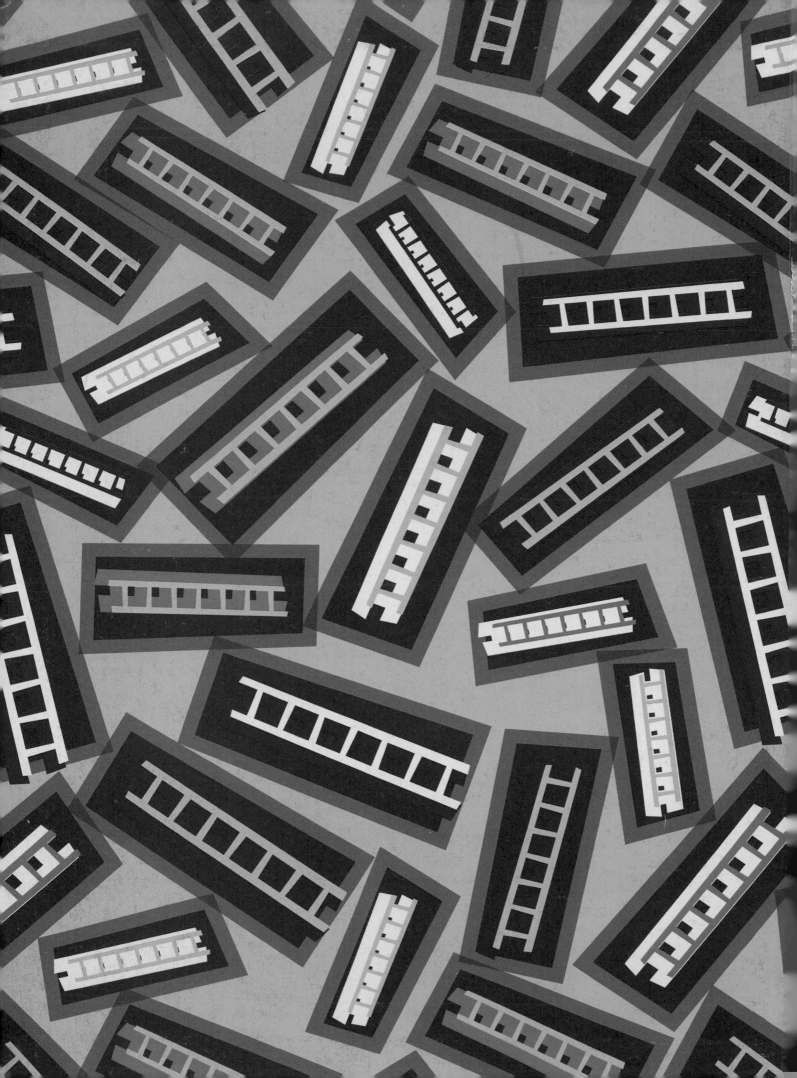